The Red Booted Chicken

Sean McLellan

AuthorHouse™
1663 Liberty Drive, Suite 200
Bloomington, IN 47403
www.authorhouse.com
Phone: 1-800-839-8640

First published by AuthorHouse 5/5/2009

ISBN: 978-1-4389-5610-7 (sc)

Library of Congress Control Number: 2009901886

Printed in the United States of America
Bloomington, Indiana

This book is printed on acid-free paper.

author house®

Dedicated to Fletcher

This book is dedicated to Fletcher, who showed me how to swim in the lake, feed the cows, and work in the garden.

Thank you, Fletcher!

I am the Red Booted Chicken from The Great State of Texas. I live on a farm with a big beautiful garden and many wonderful friends!

Texas is a great place with many land marks and grand sites to see!

I love Texas!

This is my Fancy Red Truck!

I use my Truck to feed my friends,
to haul stuff and to move trees
and plants. I also use my Truck to
work in the garden.

My Truck is the best truck
in Texas and in the world!

This is my Great and Famous Tractor!
I use my tractor in the garden to help keep
it clean and to help the vegetables grow.
It is one of the most important tools on the
farm.

I love riding my
Great Tractor!

This is my barn! I keep all of my supplies, tools and stuff in my barn. I also keep my truck and my tractor in the barn.

The barn keeps everything dry and clean.

I love my barn!

This is one of my best friends, Dallas.
He is a great dog!

Dallas loves to swim in the lake which
is on the farm. He has a lot of fun.

I love Dallas!

Fletcher who also lives on the farm, helps me. He takes me into town to pick up supplies, feed for the animals and seeds for the garden.

Fletcher is my best friend!

This is my friend Conroe. He is a Great Texas Longhorn!

Conroe is King of The Farm! We are friends and spend a lot of time together.

I love Conroe!

This is my friend Hondo The Magical frog.   He lives on a log by the lake. We are great friends and go fishing many days.

This is my friend Austin the Turtle. We are on the farm and I am teaching him how to fly. One day he will fly just like my super hero, Super Chicken!

This is my friend Lubbock the goat. He lives on the farm and eats carrots out of the garden. Some days we find our friends Tyler the Rabbit or Austin the Turtle and play. We have a lot of fun on the farm.

This is my friend Tyler The Rabbit. He also likes to eat carrots out of the garden. I am also hoping to teach him how to fly one day. Tyler told me that he would like to fly high in the sky and then swoop down and eat all of the carrots in the garden!

This is my friend Victoria the Squirrel. She loves eating pecans out of the trees. I think that she does this all day and everyday.

This is my friend Sam. We are picking apples out of the orchard in the garden. After we pick the apples, we take them down to the lake and eat them. We have a lot of fun.

This is my friend Bryan the scare crow. I helped make him with my feathers. We are picking corn together and scaring birds away.

This is my friend Fred the Armadillo. We have lots of fun on the farm. We chase the kittens and baby pigs around. Just don't tell anyone, we don't want to get caught.

In the garden is a weeping willow tree. If you look very carefully, you will find a Tutti Fruity tree.

Tutti Fruity trees have lots of candy and ice cream. This is my most favorite in the whole wide world

This is Sam making his wish for his favorite candy!

Being a true Texan means knowing your way around Texas. The first place all Texans know and love is The Alamo!

Seeing the oil wells in Texas is a must. My Grandfather owned oil wells and I can remember helping him. If you are ever in Texas, please go by and see them, you will be amazed.

This is the next site that all Texans know and love.

This is Big Tex at The Texas State Fair.

Everybody in Texas loves Big Texas.

Inspiration

This is Sam with his two dogs. He is the inspiration and the reason for writing The Red Booted Chicken.

Thank you Sam!

Lightning Source UK Ltd.
Milton Keynes UK
UKRC02n2354020217
293498UK00003B/27

9 781438 956107